A STROKE OF LUCK

THE FAMILY'S CAMPING TRIP

EVIKA BHASIN

Contents

Preface

All is sunshine and rainbows until Varun Uncle creeps in. Digging and climbing, searching and mapping in secret goes on till mother finds out. The smell of gold raps them up and takes the trio to the king and his kingdom. Making merry is impossible with the sniff of adventures around. Escaping their father's anger also is not an easy task, as the siblings are going to find out...

The book - 'A Stroke of Luck' revolves around how a pair of naughty children turn serious and look for treasure. All of this seems a myth until a game of cards turns the tables. A few findings get rapt attention and everybody remains stunned when they hear the children's story, but the problem arises when Varun Uncle suspects the pair.

This book is written by debut author Evika Bhasin, a student of Class VI, Shikshantar School. A Stroke of Luck is a delightful and lively book for children who love short adventure stories. Read this gripping adventure tale to find out what happens next and join the trio on a journey to find treasure and much more.

Acknowledgements

As an infant, I liked the airy-fairy atmosphere of fiction stories and folktales. Since I was as young as could possibly be, I used to listen to stories. As I grew up to be a toddler, I loved reading - be it the ingredients of something, a book, an advert, or a poster, I would like to read anything. I began to maintain a diary and write on various and random topics.

In the lockdown of 2020-21, I made use of this time to write stories. Seeing my interest, my parents decided to enrol me in Sara Khan Mam's Jot Down Junior Book-Writing Coaching Program. I would like to thank her for guiding me and making this book reach my hands.

Secondly, I would like to thank my parents, teachers, and family for their valuable feedback and praise. Without them, I would keep postponing this book to a later date if it was not their excitement that kept pushing and urging me to finish writing the book soon.

Thirdly, I would like to thank you, readers, who made it all possible.

Thank you so much!

About The Author

Evika Bhasin is an 11-year-old girl studying in Grade 6. She is a voracious reader, and it's very normal to see a book in her hand always. She loves penning her thoughts, be it her adventures, vacations, or sometimes just a normal day. Her favourite authors include Sudha Murthy, Enid Blyton, and Roald Dahl, to name a few. She has an interest in theatre, art, dance and writing stories and poems, and embroidery as well. She has received awards in dance and has also stood first in a national-level examination in this field.

She enjoys writing adventure stories and poems, too. Another talent that is not known to people around her is the art of voice modulation.

The inspiration behind this adventure book, A Stroke of Luck, came from a real-life incident involving herself and her watch. One day, her watch just disappeared from where she normally used to keep it. A few hours later it was declared "lost". And her sibling found "IT" a year after the incident in the most unexpected place—her own drawer. The interesting part is that the drawer had been used all those days. A sudden discovery in the most unexpected place, as one might term it, gave an idea to the story which you will read now.

CHAPTER ONE

The Family

Eva woke up to find Aki jumping on her and Bones, their dog, sniffing through the closed door. Aki and Eva often fought over every little thing, but adored each other just as much as the moon would adore the stars. Eva groaned. Akku, as Eva called him, was so naughty, yet he was obedient to his elder sister. She looked outside, then smiled. It was a beautiful morning. The sun was out in a beautiful orange colour, the hues of purple mixed with its warm rays. The flowers on the window pane danced elegantly and created lovely shadows.

Eva always wore jeans and a shirt. She was a tomboy and had deep hazel eyes and long, straight, black hair. Aki, her brother, resembled her father. He had deep black eyes which twinkled with mischief. He had curly brown hair, much to the dismay of Eva, who hated the tangles.

Bones their affectionate Pomeranian dog, with a black leather collar and brown fur coat to match it up with. They lived on a hill, in a villa. It had five bedrooms. They went to Sunflower School, which was nearby, so they just walked.

Eva smelt a fragrance from the kitchen and immediately knew something delicious was being cooked. She dashed towards it. She saw her mother busy doing magic with eggs, milk, and flour. "Oh, Mommy!" she exclaimed. "What an aromatic fragrance! What have you made for breakfast?" Mother smiled, "something you'll like," she said. "Guess"! "Umm, tough one," Eva replied. Just then, Aki came running in. "Mom has done something really exciting". he announced. Mother shook her head; with Aki, you can never be sure if he would not spill the beans. They both squealed. Mother laughed, "Oh Mum, can I eat before a bath today, please?" Eva said. "No Eva," said Mum strictly as ever. "Oh no, I guess we ought to go. We are getting lazy nowadays. Come on Aki," she said and Aki followed her upstairs.

Mum saw them and shook her head. "Nasty lot, promised themselves to give me grey hairs."

After a great deal of splashing, trying to dive and swim, fighting, and going completely crazy in the bath, they were finally exhausted and changed.

They came down to breakfast at last. In all the excitement, they had completely forgotten about their exciting breakfast. They gobbled up all their food at once. "You look like you've been hungry for ages and ages!" laughed Mum.

"We are, aren't we, Aki? Come on, or we will be late for school." "We have to reach at 7," said Mum, going suddenly serious. "Oh Mum," said Aki, knowing that he would annoy - "Sister is always early if she sleeps or wakes up, goes to school or goes playing. And she is always late if she has to come to any meal, come from school, or come from playing." Aki's eyes twinkled with mischief. Dad laughed, looking away from the newspaper. He was always amused about Aki and Eva.

"Last day of school, I cannot miss it," said Eva, eyeing Aki with eyes promising mischievous revenge.

CHAPTER TWO

Holiday Excitement

The school went on. It seemed like a really long Monday, especially after a relaxing weekend. Three o'clock rolled around, but the bus was surprisingly late. "Ugh, just what I expected," Eva grumbled to her friends. They agreed with her. She always waited for her friends to get on the bus before she walked home.

She finally reached home at 3:08 PM. Aki was waiting for her at the table. "How was school?" asked mum, while laying on the table for lunch. "Nice, I guess," mimicked Aki, before Eva could open her mouth. "I'll ask you next time I want to ask your sister something because she will not speak. Oh! close your mouth Eva I can see down till your stomach!" mum said, seeing Aki pretending to examine Eva's tongue like a doctor from the corner of her eye. "Better do your homework, Eva, it's due today," mum announced.

"Let's see what is the homework for English? Eva muttered in her room with a full stomach and satisfied remarks about her previous work. "Creative writing! Oh no! I'm horrible at that." "You'll be fine!" said dad when Eva laid down her issue. Dad was always free at this time of the day. During his break, he always visited home as his office was quite near. He was always around when Eva did her homework.

Dad and Eva together wrote a beautiful story about the summer holidays. Just then mum came in. "Have you done your packing for the summer holidays starting from tomorrow? We are going camping tomorrow. I hope you know that."

"Yes," said Eva.

"No excitement, you have nearly ticked off the entire month on your calendar, Eva, waiting for the holidays," mum exclaimed, pretending to be surprised. "Can't you be quiet Meghna? I am teaching Eva," dad said to mum, knowing that she was restless about the trip. "Oops! Sorry! I'll go to see Aki," said mum and walked out. Bones followed.

The following night was tough for the children as they were excited, but it passed soon, like every night. The next morning both Eva and Aki were up at 5:30. "Woof!" Screamed Eva and Aki. "AAH! you nearly scared me out of my wits!" shouted mum, spilling milk all over her kurta. "Oh dear!" said Aki wiping the tears of laughter as they ran down his chubby pink cheeks.

Soon dad put all the luggage safely in the boot of the red family car as they were to leave. Clothes, crockery, food, etcetera. It was a lot of luggage so much that it couldn't be stuffed into the boot so they piled some of it on top of the car and left for the camping spot.

CHAPTER THREE

The Journey Begins

They were halfway through in about 2 hours. In the large, open countryside, green grass and gigantic trees grew. Birds, butterflies, bees, and dragonflies were flying about. The peaceful chirping of crickets and birds echoed in the small hills overhead. Small saplings and flowers were a little less than in the spring, but still beautiful.

A small squirrel was running and behind it was another squirrel pretending to chop off his mate's tail. "They are playing," said Aki, fascinated, watching them gush through the car's window."

"Let's have our lunch here in the hills. It's a good place, look there's a small stream going by and it looks clean to drink from. We've bought our water bottles though," said mum, looking out of the window with Aki. They all agreed. They thought about staying there for a few days, as they liked the greenery.

After half an hour of reaching there, they were all sleeping soundly after everyone was finally stuffed. Eva woke up when she heard Bones bark at an insect. "Time to go," Eva said, looking at her watch, shaking her parents as Aki was already awake. "Nobody knows how he functions, he never sleeps," commented father on Aki, watching him play with the tame rabbits.

"It is almost twilight - after all, it has been 6 hours since we have been away from home," said mum looking at the purple sky, black, elegant birds flying north, and the stars beginning to twinkle while the moon looked shyly from behind the clouds.

They put up their tents. Eva and Aki squealed in delight as they watched the shadows play in the moonlight on the tent's cloth. Dad read them a bedtime story to make them settle down. "A long, long time ago..." a story had begun and so did the adventure. The story was about how a few characters find some treasure at the top of a mountain in a sleeping volcano's lava crater. Eva was spellbound.

Five more pages to go. Eva and Aki had fallen asleep. Eva dreamt of finding treasure at the top of the mountain, in a sleeping volcano's lava crater like that in the story. She got restless when she woke up in the morning. She awoke Aki and told him about her dream. He laughed at her. "Silly, it is a story." "Shut up, do you know how to read? Look, it says 'A true folk tale'..." said Eva. "So, you will believe it? Okay, tell me where Ali baba and the forty thieves are? Ha ha ha!" laughed out Aki.

It took a little convincing, but soon they agreed to start a secret search. They climbed on the hilltops which were not that high. They found nothing interesting, only rubbish.

During dinner, father asked them about their peculiar behaviour of climbing hilltops all day. Aki giggled at his parents' bewildered faces. Eva kicked his ankle sharply, and he stopped immediately, almost choking on what he just had by trying not to laugh. "We were just playing, Aki suggested we go climbing so..." It was Aki's turn to go red, now. "Saved", muttered Eva. "Now to prove them wrong".

CHAPTER FOUR

Dreams Of Finding Treasure

Two days passed, but they hardly knew what they were looking for. Mom had told them they were going to another camping area. "Probably we will have a better chance there," whispered Aki to Eva. It was time for them to move ahead. They reached another field, probably for campers, as a few of them were already there. "Great, you will get some friends," said Mum, looking at a few kids playing.

The next day, Eva and Aki were playing cards. Eva was losing. She put her King on Aki's 'A'. He won again. Eva was about to put down her Queen, but a sudden gust of wind blew and the card flew away and settled on a pile of dark brown fertile soil. Eva ran after her card to see where it had landed. She began to separate the soil until she caught a glimpse of gold. She saw a yellow shimmer and knew it was gold as her grandfather had told her how his father had done mining and how he identified it. She ran back to break the news to Aki, but it was supper time already.

Dad told them about Varun, his friend, and that he was going to join him. Mom was not happy, but not sad either. Both Aki and Eva had decided to not tell their parents about any findings or strange behaviour as they might not understand it, and forbid them to do so. With another grown-up hanging around, it will be much more difficult to go about their secret business without being noticed.

That night they discussed all of this in their tent, but they could not oppose dad's decision with no valid reason. They did not like Varun uncle joining them.

CHAPTER FIVE

Map To Finding Treasure

The next day, all were up early as they knew Varun uncle was to join them at ten 'o'clock. He was very particular about time.

Eva went to help her mother in the makeshift kitchen they had set up in the open air, while Aki and father went to the car to put back the tents. Mother noticed Eva's extra-grumpy face, and asked, "What happened Eva, do you not like Varun uncle joining you?" Eva hesitated. "Mom, nothing. He will bore us with his mature talks. We are younger to him, right?

Mom nodded. "Hmm, I understand. You can play while we entertain him. Please be there when he comes, though. I would like you to greet him. Eva's young hazel eyes were lighted with happiness and hope. The search wasn't far now.

Aki came back, running to Eva, who was now picking some flowers from a nearby bush and collecting them in a basket. Eva turned around, looking at Aki in surprise. Aki's round, pink face was covered with tiny droplets of sweat. The tents were probably very heavy! "Why are you so happy? Staying all day with Varun uncle is tiresome.

Moreover, we cannot even continue our search! Even though you had told me about the yellow, glittery gleams of gold you saw in the sand." Aki exclaimed gloomily. "Mom has allowed us to do whatever we want even when he is here. But we have to be there when he comes, at ten. It is 9:45 already," said Eva, watching Aki run around with excitement even though he was exhausted.

As expected, Varun uncle was there at ten. He was welcomed with the customary greeting, after which the children ran like a speeding bullet.

It was noon, and the sun was overhead. Eva and Aki were busy with their favourite pastime of late - SEARCHING for TREASURE. Separating the sand with their fingers, they found a small gold nugget alongside a gold key embedded with pearls. They sat there with their mouths hanging open. Along with it was a decorative wooden box with an elegant lock. It looked royal in its appearance. The nugget had been wrapped neatly in a velvet cloth bag embroidered with gold and silk thread.

Eva opened the locked box in which there was a piece of old paper, yellow with age. In Hindi, it had something written which said:

30 June 1576

Dear Finder,

Congratulations on the finding of the treasure.

I am a King. I live to protect my kingdom. A huge army has attacked my kingdom, and I know I won't survive the attack. Of course, if I do, I'll be very happy, but what if I don't? This thought has robbed me of my peace. I have a lot of gold, silver, ivory, pearls, jewels, etcetera. I want to keep them safe hence open the other roll of paper, which is a map. Follow the directions and you will reach my fort. The map will take you to another map, which will guide you better to my savings. Please keep my wealth in safe hands and use it for my people. My request to you is to take forward my unfulfilled dream.

His Highness King Vamana

Eva and Aki stared at each other in disbelief. Eva looked sad. She said, "Aki, this is very good news we have found the treasure, but going to the King's fort will mean telling Mom and Dad." Aki agreed with her, excited at the find and disheartened that they would need to discontinue their search.

CHAPTER SIX

Varun - Friend Or Enemy?

"What are we supposed to do now?" asked Aki. "I don't know. Going away from our campsite will obviously make everybody curious. We will not be allowed to go anywhere, which we will have to if we want to find the treasure." "We simply cannot go."

Eva and Aki ate dinner in silence. Not a word they said when Varun uncle was there. Their parents did not notice as the children feared. Varun uncle had seen the children all day, they seemed chirpy and happy. He suspected something, as they were so quiet now.

As dinner got over, Eva got up to wash her hands with the water stored in the big 20-litre bottle. Aki had a pocket in which a pouch was kept. The pouch fell, but Eva picked it up quickly. This did not escape Varun's uncle's sharp eye, though.

"You are silly," said Eva. "You should keep the pouch safe or you will lose the box and gold. Go keep it with mom's jewellery or in our tent. "Okay," said Aki and ran away.

Father was upset because the kids remained aloof during dinner. He told them when they came back, "Go, put up a tent for your uncle" "Uncle? What uncle? Oh, Varun uncle! Is he alright? Asked Eva. "Yes, why?" questioned dad. "We, being kids, can put up tents for ourselves but he, being a grown-up, cannot put a tent for himself. I wondered if he was well, that's all." Father was enraged. How could they?

Varun had overheard what Eva and Aki were talking about when Eva went to wash her hands. He had also gone to keep his dinner dishes. His head was spinning. Gold? Box? What was this? He had to investigate.

CHAPTER SEVEN

Mom Joins The Duo

The silver, bright moonlight was falling on the cloth of the tent. Eva opened the box in her tent. She examined her findings with glee.

Everyone was asleep, but Eva was still awake. She shared the tent with Aki. Mom and Dad were together with Bones sharing their tent, and Varun uncle was alone. Aki had slept.

All was quiet. The silver moon's light accompanied by the twinkling of stars. The noise of crickets and an occasional hoot of an owl echoed on the grounds. Three tents were there in a row in the north of the field. One tent on the right was alight with the light of the torch. It was Varun's tent. The light went off. Varun crept out of his tent. The chill in the wind blew on his face, tiredness vanishing. He peeped into the tent of Aki and Eva. He knew the treasure was there in the suitcase, which had a numerical lock, but he had to get to the treasure somehow.

Morning came. Eva awoke Aki. She said, "Look, the zip of the tent is open. Did you go out this morning?" Did you go out of the tent? She asked worriedly. I slept like a baby last night, replied Aki. "Well, if no one came in, and no one went out, then how did the zip open by itself? I remember zipping the tent before going to sleep." "I wonder if somebody opened the zip," said Aki. "And I wonder if that 'somebody' is our very own, dear Varun Uncle," said Eva. Aki gasped. "Aren't you talking a bit far–fetched? Varun unc..." "Don't talk nonsense, Aki. He can do anything; I feel creepy when I talk to him."

It was time for breakfast. Father and Eva were still angry with each other and mother was trying to make amends.

"Uncle, may I have the opportunity to ask you something that you may not be able to answer?" Eva asked politely. Father glared at Eva, but she ignored him completely. "Yes, please." Varun did not think she knew about yesterday. "I am obliged! As I had said, I wish to know if you were left hungry last night, by any chance?" Varun was surprised at such an ask. "No. Why?" "Just like a mouse travels to different godowns for a few grains, the same way some people, only some people, travel to different tents in the middle of the night for something they are suspicious about. I wanted to ask you, are you one of those?"

"Eva! Behave yourself! Are you accusing Varun of theft?" shouted Dad in a rage. "No Dad, I said nothing of that sort..."

"Enough! Both of you go and take your breakfast to your tent," said father. Mother looked at them with suspicion. They both got up quietly, not a word of protest, picked up their respective plates, took some extra serves, and went.

"Do you think we should tell someone?" asked Aki, who was highly impressed by Eva's 'Quick Tongue'. "We cannot search, cannot go to the fort, moreover we keep getting scolded for no fault of ours.

"Aki, Eva unzip the tent, please." "Mother? Why didn't you unzip it from outside?" "I could, but I did not. What has happened to you recently? Why are you both acting so strange?" asked mom. Aki and Eva looked at each other. Eva smiled and nodded.

"Mother, we found treasure like in the story father narrated to us, but Varun uncle knows about it, and yesterday we also noticed the open zip of the tent and strange noises that woke up my sister," said Aki." "Why did you not tell me before?" "We were afraid you may forbid us or stop us. That is the reason." Eva showed mother the nugget, pouch, box, note, and map. Mother was shocked and excited at the same time. "I will explain to your father. Let's go to the fort tomorrow," said mother.

CHAPTER EIGHT

King's Annoinment

Mother was told not to tell father about this. Everybody had decided that now was not the best time. Father was still angry, he may have forbidden them, he was chatting with Varun.

Mother had told him they were going to the nearby town to shop for groceries. Father did not suspected nothing weird or strange in this sudden trip.

The mood was exciting. "Eva, read the map. What does it say?" asked mother, "it says to cross the next hill and turn right. There we will find a tree; we have to go where it bends. After that..." "Go slow, go slow. We are barely at the bottom of the hill yet," said mother, mapping the route in her head.

It was one in the afternoon when they reached the fort. They had found the other map, as mentioned in the letter, sticking out of a doormat placed. The map was well drawn, with detailed instructions alongside the drawings.

In the fort, they saw the kitchen first. There was a small hole in the wall, which was probably for the smoke to go out. There still existed a fireplace and coal was kept in a corner. There were two large *kadhais* and plenty of big utensils. Even though the palace was old, it was well-maintained, and many things were kept, like someone was still living there. Nobody had messed up with it, after all, or there was tough security—they didn't know.

As they further explored, they found a room. There it stood, with walls once lit with *diyas* or oil lamps and decorated with marigold garlands and rose petals in a secluded corner of the area. It was peacefully quiet all around, yet it was not desolate. It stood up and looked mighty. The golden flagpole was still there despite the storms and other possible disasters in all those years. They even found silver swings in the prayer room, which were for the idols. Facing opposite, was a wooden swing, which must have been decorated well. As it was large, Eva assumed it was for the whole family to sit during religious ceremonies.

The room's walls had glass pieces that must have looked beautiful in the evening when the oil lamps were lit. They even saw the gardens, which had turned into a mini forest now. The rooms on the first floor still had fans from that time. Dirty, torn curtains hung from the high ceiling. They explored the first floor, which had beautiful dressing rooms for the king's wives and the rooms of the princess, princes, king, and queen, and other family members. The first floor also had an assembly hall or *darbar*.

The second floor had the *mehemaan kaksh* or guest rooms. The third floor had the prayer room and open area, which was divided in two. The first half for the king and his wives and the second half for the prince and his wives. The fourth floor had ministerial rooms.

The fifth floor was an artistically made terrace with marble flooring and a gold plate on which the history of the royal family was inscribed, hung on the wall.

Eva and her family looked at the palace in awe. What lives of luxury the royal family enjoyed!

As per the map, the wealth was supposed to be in the assembly hall. The trio reached the grand wooden doors which had lions etc. carved out of bamboo wood. They entered the assembly hall and felt like a royal person. There were many silver seats now black with age. Straight ahead was a golden throne that was for the king. Eva's sharp eyes saw rusted metal trumpets near the door. She could imagine the sudden news of losing the battle and everybody running to shelter. The palace was in that very state.

Aki ran to sit on the throne. "Aki nooo..." Eva shouted and stopped. The moment Aki sat on the throne, it toppled over and a huge Chester opened, which was overflowing with rubies and jewels and jewellery and emeralds. Everybody froze. Six eyes feasted on the site. But a new worry crept up their minds: how were they supposed to carry the treasure home?

"Welcome," said a voice. They turned to look. A boy, not more than 21, was standing there. He wore a simple dhoti and a white kurta. "I am Abhimanyu. I assume you found the treasure." Abhimanyu quickly told them about his village and that all the villagers were descendants of the king. That is why they could not find the treasure. "Every day a villager comes to maintain the palace and hopes someone would find the wealth."

In a jiffy, the villagers gathered around and took the treasure to the sarpanch or *mukhya*. The trio accompanied them.The sarpanch was overjoyed. He promised Eva to keep the treasure safe and crown Abhimanyu the next king as he was there on the day the treasure was found. This is what their ancestors had told them.

Father was shocked when he heard this. He apologised to them and sent Varun back home. They then decided to stay in the village for the next seven days before they had to return home. Father scooped up Bones and Eva and Aki ran to pack their bags. Time for the last part of the adventure.

For John
Now And Forever

"Today Is A Gift.
That's Why We
Call It
The Present."

AA Milne

"First You Are Young.
Then Middle-Aged.
Then You Are Old.
Then You Are Wonderful."

Alice Roosevelt Longworth

JETTY BOY

Alone, but not alone.
The waves are vigorous.
They speak to me.
Very strong ebb and flow.
Yet, there is silence.
In my head.
Alone with the ocean.
Sitting on huge rocks.
Way out into the sea.
All I need is right here.
I close my eyes.

Breathe in the salty air.
Smile.
I sit alone in my "playground".
I am eleven years old.
Will life ever be this good again?
Yes.

Mr. and Mrs. Straus

They have had their "playground" days.
Mr. Straus owned Macy's department store.
He played well. And won well.
Rich, but not pretentious.
Ida and Isidor are in love.
Have been for many years.
On the deck of the Titanic.
1912.
Cold clear night.
Iceberg ahead.
It was spotted too late.
Strangely, they have no fear.
They have one another.
That is all that matters.
Drinking champagne in crystal glasses.
They think of their wedding day.
A celebration.
They will stay together.
Women and children first.
She chooses to stay with her man.
"I am a very old woman," she says.
"I will not leave Mr.Straus now."
Or ever.
Still in love.
Now and forever.
We "play" to the end.

LOVE NEVER DIES

A man sits in his playground.
In a wheelchair.
Quiet.
Just stares ahead.
Has end stage dementia.
An old man, but still romantic.
A lady comes along in her wheelchair.
She pulls in next to the man.
Slowly, oh so slowly, the man puts his
Hand over the ladies right hand.
Still looking ahead.
Both of them.
Not a word is spoken.
Yet, there is a connection.
Romance at a nursing home?
You bet.
Happiness: Assured.
Love never dies.

SHOW UP

I once was in a playground for an event that I did not want to attend, but my friends organized this and I had to show up.

A close friend and I had been having a rough time of it. We were being nasty to one another. I cannot remember why. But it had to stop. The anger had to go away.

So my friends organized an after school fight. Now picture this: two scrawny boys who had never fought in their lives were called to the playground to punch each other out.

We did. We hit each other hard, not really knowing how to do it. Probably looked stupid, but the crowd cheered us on.They were coaching us.Was there injury: probably. But we survived. And we bonded once again. And we grew up.

A playground. Just show up.

No winner that day.

But we played the game.

PLAY

Those halcyon days of being a kid.
I want to hold onto them.
Even at the age of 78.
Perhaps now, more than ever.
I never thought of what would be ahead.
Just did my thing.
I was an odd kid.
My brother called me a brat.
Guess there was some truth in that.
Did fine in elementary school.
Not in kindergarten.
Can you flunk kindergarten?
I almost did.
The teacher, very tall and stern.
She did not like me at all.
Smelly mat on the floor.
Not for me.
Milk, not for me.
Just get on with it.
Then first grade happened.
I was in love with Miss Price.
She "got" me.
I was home.
Her room was a playground.
Playgrounds can be inside or out.
They can be large or small.
They can be anything at all.

As long as you can "play" there.
Be yourself.
Discover who you are.
And dream.
And I did.
Graduated. Cool!
Onto high school
Met a girl and fell in love.
She wanted to marry.
I was 16 and not ready.
We dated.
And discovered New York City.
Talk about a playground.
NYC is a gigantic playground.
And Broadway was OUR street.
Saw a bunch of shows.
Tickets were around $3.00!
Good seats, too.
Lunch was only $2.50.
Really swanky place.
Then back to New Jersey.
College.
Now that WAS a playground.
First intimate times.
With a boy.
Yes, I'm a boy (now a man).
Had a feeling I was gay.
Did not know what that was.
So I still dated girls.
Had my pick.

I was thin and cute.
So they told me.
Wow. Did we play!
One night in a cemetery.
It was the place to go.
Moonlight. Just two of us.
Bliss.
Happiness.
Cemetery=Playground.
Strange, but true.
Graduate school.
It was easy.
Girls, boys, yummy.
A gigantic field of fun.
Next: taught in a university.
Each classroom was my playground.
The best classes were raucous, joyous.
And then, one night, I met HIM.
At a club.
We spotted one another.
Cute, both of us.
Available, both of us.
And then I learned something.
If you feel something, SAY IT.
For two hours we looked at one another.
Not a word spoken.
And then.
And then.
He said it.
"Can I do anything for you?"

What if he had not said it?
But he did.
John and I were together 46 years.
A "playground" just for two.
Come with me to the playground.
It can be a field, an arena, any space.
Amazing things to discover.
Let me cheer you on.
Let me be your coach.
Just be willing to play.

PLAYING

It's not about winning or losing.

It's about showing up and playing.

Many people, wiser than I, wrote catchy messages about "play". GK Chesterton: "The true object of all human life is play."

George Bernard Shaw: "We don't stop playing because we grow old. We grow old because we stop playing."

"Play is the royal road to childhood happiness and adult brilliance." J.C. Pearce.

Martin Buber: "Play is the exultation of the possible." Plato: "Life must be lived as play."

And my favorite: A child at play is like "seeing an artist paint, for in play a child says things without uttering a word." Erik Erikson.

Playing.

Together.

A girl and a boy.

Not much of a playground.

But they made it work.

And they smiled.

No toys.

So they made them.

From scraps of paper.

From a twig or two.

From imagination.

And they played.
Without fear.
Together.
And then they stopped.
Went their separate ways.
Never to meet again??
Off to another country.
America.
Married their spouses.
Had children of their own.
The spouses passed away.
Guess what happened.
The two kids, now "old", met again.
Fell in love.
Married.
Like a novel?
You see, the kids were Jewish.
They met in a concentration camp.
Fast forward to 1945.
American forces liberated the camp.
The kids were separated.
Never to be seen again?
Well, you now know the story.
It all started with play.
In a terrible place.
But they created their own playground.
And it kept them focused.
On hope.
Keep your focus.

JETTY TALKS, #1

So many times over the years I have remembered that jetty where I sat on the hard rocks and listened to the waves telling me stories. Better than any classroom I could have been in.

And then this happened: I studied Shakespeare, taught it in a high school before going on to university teaching. In fact, one of my favorite moments as a new teacher happened in that high school sitting in the faculty room as a newbie and knowing, somehow, not to open my mouth, just listen.

So, the old timers were going on about students. One asked me what groups I would be teaching: "I have two 3 levels and one 1 level". "Oh, you won't be able to do anything with the 3's. Just babysit them."

I said nothing. Just shut up.

And then I did what I wanted to do: I taught the 3's the play "Romeo And Juliet." And at the same time brought in moments and songs from "West Side Story."

And then went further.

I staged scenes from both the play and the musical in an outdoor playground.

Well, these 3's became 1's. Totally engrossed in the work of learning Shakespeare, they soared. Beautiful young high school kids taking on new self esteem.

And most got A's for their work.

So, back to jetty boy and the waves: what was really happening there was a lesson from nature William Shakespeare had written so many years before:

"And this, our life,

Exempt from public haunt,
Finds tongues in trees,
Sermons in stones,
Books in the running brooks,
And good in everything.
And I would not change it."

That said, I will occasionally introduce in these pages "Jetty Talks": things I have "found" and want to pass along to you. Kind of like TED talks, but shorter and personalized just for you.

Here is the first one. Those two kids in the "playground" they made while in the concentration camp: they were vulnerable.

They did not know the word, perhaps, but they knew the feeling.

I spoke of this concept in my book "Kicked In The Ass Hard, And Still Here". It bears repeating in this book about finding and holding happiness:

Vulnerability=clarity=power.

Simple.

Hold onto that idea.

I am sure it will surface again.

SAY IT

Just want to SAY this to you: sometimes we can miss the best opportunities if we do not speak up. C.S. Lewis wrote about connecting with people: one of the joys of his life.

For me, when I meet a person for the first time I will see if they feel like talking. Why not? Talk is free.

And we are not on a phone or a laptop, we are face to face. Cool. We begin to chat.

And what happens? As C.S. Lewis noted: "you, too, I thought I was the only one."

Common ground feels good. If we did not "say it", there would be no common ground. Time and time again I found new friends this way.

One day there was a biker dude with long white hair, a tie dye shirt, lots of tats. With a lady of course. I SAY to him: "I like your shirt." Dude: "she doesn't like it."

But, that's OK with him. "We're not married so I can do what I like." And he smiled and was gone. He was just fine doing it his way in his playground space.

The same day a lady of some years, and very pretty, says to me: "I love your shoes." Was wearing my orange crocs (so comfortable). "Those shoes are so sexy" she went on. Ah. I guess we had a really nice connection for about two minutes, and never saw her again.

My point is this: SAY IT! Be sincere, don't force yourself into someone's space unless you get the feeling you are being invited.

If John had not said "can I do anything for you?" our history would have been unclaimed.

I like how it worked out. And, wow, we played.

IMAGINE

Thinking back to the boy on the jetty named Jay, I got this: my feeling of freedom was fantastic. I could be me, and that was enough.

Imagination, to Einstein, was a key to life. He wrote: "Imagination is everything. It's the preview to life's coming attractions." I did not realize, on that jetty, what imagination was; had never heard the word. But I had it.

And I imagine that is what motivated me to get to that jetty whenever I could. Dropped off the school books, walked to the ocean and became whatever kids are meant to become.

And I have never lost my sense of wonder from that early age.

I invite you, right now, to close your eyes and SEE the kid in you once again. What were you doing? What made life happy for you. Revisit those images often.

Fun: on a cave wall there was some writing. Translated it was "help, I want to be happy, and this cave is not working for me." OK, I made it up, but you get the point. Find the "cave" that works for you.

Why this obsession with having a "man" cave or a "woman" cave or a "kid" cave? You know the answer: we all need our personal, private space to create, a bit better, who we are. What goes on in your cave is no one's business. Unless you are doing something that will impact your life in a negative way.

Make wise choices. But make them. Zing! (I love that word). Your life, your way, your space. Close the door, turn on the twinkle lights. STOP. BE QUIET. Find the joy and never let it go. Zing!

FIND YOURSELF

On a tree.

A sign:

"I come here to find myself."

Magic in those words.

I was just climbing a mountain.

Did not expect words of wisdom.

Unexpected joy.

Total silence on that path.

No cell phones.

No loud crowds.

Beauty and calm.

I started to breathe better.

Slept under the stars that night.

William Shakespeare: he was my first playwright as an actor. My role: Puck, or Robin Goodfellow, in "A Midsummer Night's Dream." I was painted all in green makeup, head to toe. I looked like a big can of peas.

My acting career would take a detour for many years until I had enough money saved from university teaching to get my Actors' Equity card and become legitimate.

And make a decent income from performing, something my orthodox grandfather told me not to do: "you will be a bum, living under a bridge somewhere; no, NO acting." When I became successful he had a different tune; but I did get his point.

After all, I needed to PLAY in some space, some playground or arena that would pay me to do what I most enjoyed. I was lucky. The dream came true.

Actor Martin Landau told of his experience: "A good director makes a playground and allows you to play." A good coach does that for you as well.

So, I found myself. Yet I had no idea why this would shape my life so much. Until one night, many years later, in Utica, New York.

Doing the Broadway show "Cabaret" on tour all over the USA and Canada.

Opening night party.

Noisy.

Crowded.

Silly.

Not for me.

I took my friend to the top balcony.

Deserted theater, 3000 seats.

Only a ghost light on the stage.

Shadows all over the gothic space.

Silence.

We just sat there.

A fantastic sanctuary.

Two hours ago I was on that stage.

I was playing.

And getting paid to do it.

Life from the jetty to this.

Takeaway: Use your talents to grow.

Use your talents to inspire.

Use your talents to make others happy.

Use your talents to create your playground.

JETTY TALK #2

My father, Morris, was fascinating to me. I did not know it when I was a kid, I just had a sense that my dad was very cool.

Unlike some of the other fathers in the neighborhood who abused their kids verbally and physically, Morris only put his hands on me to mess up my hair. He was playful. And silly at times. Life was not easy in the 1950's. Yet he made it OK for the family and never, never complained.

And he said often: "never worry about anything."

So that takes me to the word FEAR. Something to get rid of. Bulldoze it away. As Franklin Roosevelt said: "we have nothing to fear but fear itself."

Some people who experience fear in a big way (and this is VERY real), stop playing. Their choice, perhaps, but not a healthy or healing one.

And some will find the following not to their liking, but here goes anyway.

One of the things that people fear is "death". In fact, one of the great moments from the film "Moonstruck" happens this way: the wife learns of an affair her husband is having with a rather common woman, a lady with very expensive taste. He buys her all kinds of jewelry and other toys.

Wife wonders: why do men do this?

Someone says to her: it's because some older men fear death.

Ah, so is the "playing" that some men engage in a way to cheat death?

Well, here's the answer I give: WE DO NOT DIE. So why fear it. Oh, yes, we leave our bodies. That is inevitable for a variety of reasons. But please "play" with this thought: there is plenty left of ourselves after leaving the body.

I often attend an ashram. It is a playground for me: great beauty, great food, great new people to learn from, and amazing peace and quiet in the country.

A guru (a spiritual leader) suggested these words: I AM. And I always WILL BE. And I do not need a body to BE. I am writing these thoughts from memory, so I may not be fully accurate.

But here's the point: you and I have experienced loss in our lives.

And when I lost my husband, John, it was one of the most vulnerable moments of my life. And yet, I soldiered on. And I got this: so much remains from a life well lived. The body may be gone. The spirit, the connection, the guidance, the clarity never goes away. That is something to celebrate.

With that in mind: it is vital to keep playing, creating, finding happiness in all the unexpected places. Show up. Do things that might feel a bit scary. You are your own special creation.

This may seem like something out of the twilight zone but it happened: one night I was watching something funny on "The Golden Girls" and started to laugh.

At that moment I "got" that it was not my usual laugh at all. It was John's very specific, special laugh. It just happened. And it still does. Life, and the gifts of life, goes on.

Those moments of clarity are powerful.

Hold onto them.

KATE'S PLAYGROUND

She was fired. A few times. It was a wake up call to her. She just wanted to act. Jobs came easily, and some went away easily. She had to do better and she did. Oscars, other awards.

So what. She was a "so what" gal.

What made her life "zing" was the playing. Not the money. We only need the money to take care of our needs.

Too many people worship money. Kate

Hepburn didn't. And get over this thing about never having enough. We spend too much.

I was on a tour with a show and a lovely, tall, lady who had been a dancer at Radio City Music Hall in NYC was carrying on: "I have no money left and I just got paid."

Well, yes, she was making a lot of money in this show. And once the paycheck happened, she spent a lot of time at the bar (fine, if that is your thing) and before she knew it, a hundred dollars evaporated. Then off to the mall the next day. Another hundred dollars. You get the point.

Back to Kate Hepburn. Did you ever notice her hair: she just let it alone. The woman had her own style. And she was magnificent.

She did a film that came out in 1938 called "Holiday". You need to see this movie. "Thanks, coach!"

Imagine this:

A mansion.

Very wealthy, boring family.

Kate's character, Linda Seton, was having none of it.
She loved her independent lifestyle.
Did it her way.
Party downstairs in the ballroom.
She did not attend.
Instead, she created a playground.
Top floor of the mansion.
All hers. Bonbons, champagne.
Toys, piano, fireplace, a trapeze.
She was happy, almost ecstatic.
Just needed to be left alone.
The snobs in the family did not "get" her.
One thing was missing:
A man who could really love her.
She found him.
But the guy was engaged to her sister.
Sister finally dumped the guy.
She was so artificial.
He was 100% real.
Just like Kate's character.
They fell in love.
Went off on an ocean voyage.
And you just know: they played together.
End of story.
Takeaway: Be yourself. Know what you want.
Go out and get it.

YOUR WAY

I could have been boring: the kind of dude who sits on a couch and whines all day. Not for me. My advice: find YOUR playground and things can change.

When I was a kid, the jetty days, I took myself to a little movie theater in my small beach town and got in for about 25 cents.

That included a small popcorn, cartoons, the movie and an exit gift (for free) of a coffee mug or a dessert dish, that kind of thing.

My life changed even more in that theater (truly a playground!). So this is what happened:

Auntie Mame.

Who?

Auntie Mame.

The name of the movie.

Starring Rosalind Russell.

Who?

Look her up on youtube.

Lights dim.

The movie begins.

My life is about to change.

Technicolor!

New at the time.

Insane jewels on a stylish wrist

That was the first image.

Then a NYC penthouse apartment.

A party was in progress.

Zing!
Who could be this rich?
Well, she was.
But that was not the point.
She knew what was important.
And it was not the money.
Until she lost it all.
Stock market crash of 1929.
Along came Beau.
She fell in love.
He was "in oil".
She was set for life.
Until Beau took a picture.
And fell down a mountain.
Gone.
She still was rich.
Now what?
She wrote a book.
She continued to "play".
What counted most?
Her friends.
Her connectivity.
Her generosity.
One night, she was so broke.
But put her last quarter in a Salvation
Army kettle.
She knew how to live.
She said "life's a banquet."
Wow.
I wanted to be her.

Have nice things.
But, above it all, be free to be me.
Mame did it.
You can do it, too.
Ask.
Ask "who am I?"
"Why am I here?"
"What do I want?"
We will revisit this later.
Takeaway: Be "curious."
That word is golden.

JETTY TALK #3

"Napoleon Dynamite."
    A film about a skinny, tall dude.
    He has few friends.
    He is a bit awkward.
    So what.
    He has his playground.
    No other kids around to bother him.
    Just a metal pole with a ball on a string.
    He spends his recess time with that ball.
    Tossing it around on that string.
    Delightfully engaged in play.
    He needs nothing else.
    He is just fine.
    Content.
    Satisfied.
    OK.

Napoleon IS the playground.
    Wait! What is Jay saying?
    This is too bizarre.
    Or is it?
    I don't think it is bizarre at all.
    We are born.
    We create every day.
    We learn who we are.
    We embrace our playfulness.

Our happiness.
We become the playground.
Simply: we organize the playground.
We direct what happens there.
We open it and close it.
We choose our "toys."
We choose our paints.
We choose what to do.
Happiness follows.

A woman I knew stopped playing.
    Just sat.
    Day after day.
    Stayed in the house.
    Got bitter.
    Lost her friends.
    Lost her life.
    Unlock your gate.
    Find within you the "secret garden".
    It is your arena.
    It is your field.
    It is your playground.

It just comes alive when you let it.
    So why not let it.
    Buddha said something like this: your life is a raft. Lovely
image.
    I say your life is a playground.

Let it be.
You ARE the playground.

DISNEY!

They were screaming!
With happiness.
A huge audience.
We took our bows.
And the screaming was deafening.
We loved it.
I was playing Maurice, Belle's dad.
The show: "Beauty And The Beast."
The Disney version.
Dozens of little girls in the audience.
All dressed in gorgeous Belle gowns.
Then we met a lot of them after the show.
Euphoric is the word that comes to mind.
And parents, too, loved that show.
Everyone was happy.
Disney on stage.
The transformation at the end: magic.
The beast becomes human.
Belle was already loving the beast.
And then the beast turns into a prince.
He is gorgeous.
Belle is gorgeous.
The world is gorgeous.
And to think I got paid to do this.
Eight times a week.
Sometimes nine.
We were totally sold out.

We had to do more shows.
Disney: magic!
Grab it. Hold it.

THE BIG PLAYGROUND

"Anything can happen if you let it." My favorite line from "Mary Poppins." When we needed a mood enhancer John and I would go off to the New Amsterdam Theater on Broadway, buy our usual box seats and watch the show. Holding hands, I suspect, as we were a very romantic couple.

Always fun. But we always got the same box for one reason: Mary passed right by us as she flew up to the sky at the end of the show. Magic! I suspect we cried. Disney on Broadway has become a marvelous tradition.

Yet, for so many, the theme parks have become transformative. I will say right now: they are the best playgrounds in the world.

Why?

The colors are magical.

The lights are magical.

The rides are magical.

Even the turkey legs are magical.

Gigantic turkey legs for sale.

Not sure if they still have them.

When I first went there, I ate one.

Not sure if I finished it. Huge.

Whenever I go back to Disneyland, I become a six year old again. They call it the happiest place on earth. It is also one of the most expensive playgrounds on earth. So what! I cannot imagine a world without Disney or Disneyland. So we pay the price.

Walt Disney wrote: "Laughter is timeless. Imagination has no age, and dreams are forever."

And then there was my mother.

She wanted to see Disneyland.

John and I invited my parents, Betty and Morris, to Orlando, got them a swell room in a round hotel, and off we went.

The fun began as Mickey played with Betty while she giggled shamelessly. But when Grumpy came to her, my mother was "reborn."

I think Grumpy was tickling her, sidling up to her, causing her happiness level to reach a new life peak. She was in love with Grumpy. She was in love with life.

All around there were kids in strollers, men and ladies in wheelchairs and walkers. All ages, shapes and sizes and ethnic backgrounds. What was happening? They were all playing. Joy everywhere.

When you wish upon a star, your dreams come true.

BROADWAY

They call Broadway in NYC the street of dreams. Some say that for every light on Broadway there is a broken heart. You simply have to see it to believe it.

Broadway has become the biggest theater and entertainment street in the world. Actually a lot of streets make up what is referred to as Broadway.

And when you say you are working on Broadway as a performer or an usher or a janitorial assistant you could be working in any one of over 40 large playhouses.

And making a lot of money. Exactly as it should be. The minimum salary,at last check, for a performer doing eight shows a week was around $2500. And up. Stars can command a quarter of a million a week. And some of them get it.

Big news: a lot of Times Square has become a mall. Playground! Plenty of tables, street performers, shops, fantasies, excitement. Some dance in the streets.

I did. One night. I was dating this guy who was a dean in a college somewhere in the midwest. Cute. Tall. Thin. A keeper. I took him to see "Hello, Dolly".

It had snowed while the show was going on. We left the St. James theater; 44th. Street was deserted. No cars in sight. Fresh snow on the ground.

I won't get into how the evening ended. That's for another book. (It was really memorable).

We looked at one another, and started dancing in the snow. Cool. Actually it was freezing cold out there, but we got warmed up when we danced. I can always say I danced on Broadway!

Street of dreams, jobs, auditions and rejections. Big star, small star, no star: we all went through the same stuff. I was there at the right time as I got many jobs.

Some in NYC, most on tour or in theaters around the USA. Fun. Hard work. But fun.

So, Broadway really is like no other place for the zillions of happy feet that have walked over the streets in Times Square. It isn't the magic kingdom of Disney. But it has magic. Fantasy. Undeterred enthusiasm.

It brings thousands of people to one location each week. And it is the stuff that dreams are made of. A playground? Indeed it is.

TIMES SQUARE: DESERTED

If you ever stood in Times Square you will have memories of lights, thousands of people enjoying the "playground" that is Broadway. Jolly. Silly. Amazed. Wow!

Imagine it all gone.

No people.

No traffic.

No lights.

No shows.

Unimaginable?

John and I were standing at the corner of Broadway and 46th. Street.

Silence.

Smoke was engulfing us.

The world had come to an end.

Or so it felt.

The twin towers had just fallen.

The wind had brought the thick smoke all the way uptown. Dozens of blocks.

There were no words to be spoken.

In a way, it was bound to happen.

When we get complacent as a people or in ourselves, we might need a wake up call.

9/11 woke us up. And the reality for young and old hit us hard. Collectively. We needed to find one another again: goodness,the calm,the faith in ourselves and others.

John and I found the gathering we needed. As Broadway slowly came back to life, the people slowly came back to

Broadway. We knew we had to connect: so we went to the theater. There, a thousand or more people can connect.

Talk about a playground: a theater is a playground for the actors, backstage people, ushers, box office staff, cleaners. If you believe that cleaners in a theater, or anywhere, are just holding mops, or brooms or rags: think again.

They are dancing to their own rhythm as they enjoy their work and I have seen this first hand. The best workers in a theater "playground" love their work. They can't wait to get there. And, not to be too poetic, the work space can be a sanctuary.

Takeaway: Get out of the house and join the rest of us seeking clarity. Stuff happens.

When we find clarity, and we will, we are among the powerful. It can take patience and strength. Once we get there, it feels so good to meet others who are seeking the same energy: something we can share.

There are a million "playgrounds" to explore. Start with your own. You are the conductor!

CURTAIN UP

I have written of this night once before in the memoir "Finding Myself At The Stage Door." If you like actors and theaters you might enjoy that book. This story is worth repeating here.

John and I got tickets for "The Music Man."

What could be more natural in an unnatural time. Small town Americana with small town values, decency, fun, and kids learning to play musical instruments. Could they play?

None of them knew how. But they played all right.

So, the curtain goes up on "The Music Man" on Broadway and, presto, the mood in that place was happy. Then it was joyous. Then it was euphoric. Ecstatic.

The audience bonded from the outset: this was the cathartic moment we ALL needed in this historic playhouse. Play. A beautiful word. Musical play: even better.

All went well.

And then the finale.

The moment we all waited for.

The moment we all needed.

We were, in that playground of a theater, all the peoples of the world, all backgrounds, all ages, all ethnicities, all sexual orientations, religious or not religious, all hopeful. All tired from the days before. And now all being brought back to life.

Together.

Picture this: as the cast is about to sing the main song, "Seventy Six Trombones", a dozen or more kids playing instruments are on stage doing what they thought they could never do, but they did. Wait. It gets better.

A gigantic American flag comes into view at the back of the stage. It comes down from what are called the "flies", that area above the stage that holds the scenery, lighting poles, magic things.

The biggest American flag we ever saw.

We all, in that audience, just lost it.

And we found it.

Together, we began to sing "God Bless America." Americans, Indian people, Asian, British, Turkish, Mexican, everyone together, at the top of our lungs.

John and I held hands, we cried, we were shaking. We had come home. No matter what chaos there is in the world, and there always has been and always will be, there is always a sanctuary for us: a playground, an arena, a field.

We have a chance to dust off the "stuff" that can take away our joy and sing, and dance. "God Bless America", that hopeful and loving song by Broadway composer Irving Berlin, took us to a better place. The audience members near us started to hold hands: strangers holding hands.

How did that make us feel? Connected! Loved! Safe! Optimistic! Beautiful!

We became ONE, and we became STILL. Yes, there was music and dancing and crazy happiness all over, on stage and off. Yet, there was a stillness in that place.

When the final curtain came down, we looked at one another and knew we had witnessed a new day. People who had no knowledge of one another a few hours before were now hugging.

Tears of joy flowed.

Without thinking about it, we had all come here, at this moment, to find ourselves again. We had come to "The HAPPINESS Playground."

Indeed: we came and we met and we connected and we soared. I know it might seem a bit "much" yet I believe that night added some more days to our lives: happiness is healthy. Endorphins flow in the body.

Ain't Broadway grand!

CAMP

How can I get out of here?
    Please let me escape.
    I can find a way to a bus stop.
    It might be miles away.
    I don't care.
    Help!
    I cannot do this!
    I am not an athlete.
    I am an actor of sorts.
    Why am I here?
    Camp.
    The ultimate playground for kids.
    And for adults if they see it that way.
    I saw it as "hell" that first night.
    Will the sun ever come up?
    I did not sleep.
    The morning came.
    And suddenly, I was not alone.
    And I felt better.

I was scrawny, gay, from New Jersey. As some might say, and forgive this, I was "f*cked".

But not for long. I was hired in this wilderness setting to assist in the theater program. That I could do. Paint scenery, hang it, be a merry little gay elf doing my thing as long as I was not too "out there".

So I behaved and started to feel useful. The food was good, really good. The people were nice. And Barry, my co-counselor (gorgeous guy, tall, thin, blonde) was really friendly to me. He was a true athlete.

I watched him and learned a little about being more "butch": it really came from being confident. Barry was a great coach and cheerleader for me. The days went on and I felt more and more that I belonged in this playground.

And I did. Before the end of that summer season in the hills of Pennsylvania, I grew as a human being. I led the "color war" singing event for my team (each of two teams had a different color: blue, orange perhaps) and we did athletic stuff, theater stuff, all the things kids do.

Except only one team could go on to victory. We won the singing event. Nice.

Well, my check bounced. I got home and put it in the bank. Bounced. My grandfather took care of that. It did not deter me from other camps in other places.

Salvation Army camp, another sports camp, a theater camp (from which people like Jon Cryer, Robert Downey, Natalie Portman and dozens of other kids who became stars found themselves). All together I spent over 25 years helping to raise kids.

All in playgrounds. Camp: a true playground. And it was in the Salvation Army camp that I almost lost my virginity.

Almost. There was a very lovely, smart and horny European gal there. We had fun together.

One night she arranged for the staff lounge, up a hill, to be available just for us. She looked beautiful. We kissed. We hugged. We.

Wait, we didn't do the "deed". Oh she wanted to, very much. All the way, as they say. Something in me said: STOP! I am not ready to be a father.

I was only a kid. An eighteen year old kid.

But still a kid. I wanted to play some more.

What a camp. It was there that I saw the sign on the tree up the mountain: I come here to find myself. I did just that.

Camp is, for many, the ultimate playground.

That night in the staff house with Maria, I played. I won because I knew what I wanted, what I did not want, and who I was. She understood. We remained friends. I would never become a father in the usual sense. John and I never had kids.

When people ask me: "do you have children" I blush a bit. Yes, I could have had. And I answer this way: "I have helped to raise thousands of kids." And it was true. A total joy in my life.

Takeaway: Do something that scares you. Eleanor Roosevelt told us that. Know who you are, and who you are not. Climb a mountain if you can. You are never too old to play.

JETTY TALK #4

Dream.
Just allow a dream to happen.
One way to do this is to sleep well.
Someone said to me: "I don't feel human."
Why? I asked.
"I don't sleep."
Being a friend and a coach, I tried to help.
If we have no sleep, we have no energy.
Without energy, we can "play" but not well.
My advice to my friend:
Get the best mattress you can afford.
No more "mr. lumpy, or mr. too soft."
Or mr. too hard.
And keep your bedroom space cooler.
Too hot may keep you awake.
Get a fan.
Get a sound machine.
They are about $20.00.
Well worth the investment.
Waves, storms, rain, crickets.
Just push a button.
And make your room very dark.
Get the insulated darkening curtains.
And a fantastic comforter.
Something "comforting" over me is key.
Now here is something to try: cover your eyes when you
sleep.

Just do not cover your nose!

They make eye covers.

You might want to get one.

You might not fall asleep right away. So try this: open the "valve" on the top of your head. OK, I know there is not a physical valve. Just try this: Use three fingers gently, and I mean very gently,to massage the top of your head in a circular way. Maybe for 15 seconds.

Then, breathe fully and deeply.

Then, stretch each finger of your right hand and then your left hand. Slowly. You should be more calm by now. If you yawn,something good is happening. Trust me.

And here is the thing that usually "does it" for me: I select an image. Always the same image. This is something I find comforting from my past or present. Not a person. A thing. This is very personal. And always the same. I can be part of the image or not. I choose to be in the frame of the image.

And then I add a vocal sound. It can be anything, but not loud. A number, a hum, anything that goes along with making you more calm.

I am usually asleep by then.

You will find your own way.

The way is a form of play.

You create it.

Never divulge to anyone your image or the sound you have chosen. They are yours.

Hold onto them. Yes, this is also a form of "play." Healthy, healing, calming play. Not too energetic. That is the point.

WE ARE NOT MACHINES

In Amsterdam.

Something was happening.

Not a clue.

Went to the hospital.

Hepatitis.

Isolated for three weeks.

What caused this?

I found out.

A doctor had given me an antibiotic.

A huge dosage.

Ruined my immune system.

Thanks, doc.

It all turned out fine. Took myself to Paris and sat on my balcony and tried not to think about anything. I had learned my lesson. We are not machines. The body can only do so much before it shuts down in one way or another.

Not only had I been directing a huge play with 50 actors, I was also cramming for my doctoral exams and the defense of my dissertation. Got through all of that, barely. And then the hepatitis.

We wake up, go to work, eat, sleep, repeat. The word "play" does not appear in that list. It needs to be there.

Years later, I had a flu of some kind. It knocked me out for three weeks. My doctor was wonderful when I asked why this was happening. Her answer: we are not machines.

Things happen. Hydrate,a lot of water, rest and calm down. If playing were to happen it would be with simple exercise: walking, doing the dishes by hand, making my bed, stretching. I got better quickly.

Everything in moderation.

Takeaway: My father always said "if something is broken, get it fixed." He was always a cheerleader, a coach, a wise and loving man. I just did not realize it at the time. Now I do. Thanks, Dad.

DINOSAUR

I was running around the house.
    Making a lot of noise.
    Having the best fun.
    I was a dinosaur.
    The greatest, most powerful dinosaur.
    "Stop it! Just stop it.
    You are not a dinosaur."
    This from my mother.
    I went outside.
    Did the same thing.
    Even louder.
    Mother grabbed my dinosaur costume.
    That was the end of that.
    Fast forward.
    Graduated from college.
    Became an accountant.
    Hated it.
    Did it until I retired.
    Dementia set in.
    One day I got into the car.
    Forgot something.
    Went in the house to get it.
    Had not put the car into "park."
    It rolled down the hill.
    My wife saved the day, and the car.
    We had great love for one another.
    Went to the river for a day.

She knitted.

I went to the edge of the river.

My cane steadied my walking.

Stood there.

I smiled.

Memory.

Of the dinosaur.

Cut to an image of my wife on her bench.

Back to the river.

I was no longer there.

I had returned to nature.

I became a dinosaur.

Smiling because that all happened in a film I was in called "Dinosaur." One of those independent films where you make almost no salary, but you eat very well and sleep in the best lodging. And meet great people.

A film set is a miracle of a playground for actors, technical staff, editors, cooks and caterers, and a bunch of people who just show up and make it all work. Genius.

My takeaway from "Dinosaur": play all that you can. Be a dinosaur, a monkey, a frog, a butterfly, a princess, a train conductor, a tree, an ocean, a playground. Just BE.

JETTY TALKS #5

I panicked.
    Just like the first night I was in a camp.
    The night I tried to escape and just stayed.
    I just decided to stay.
    And I stayed 25 years.
    Almost 57 years later I met Donald.
    John had "left his body"; I needed a friend.
    Donald became a wonderful friend.
    I was going to buy a house in his community.
    Put down the deposit.
    Started to get decorating ideas.
    And panicked.
    What was I doing in a place called Ocala?
    Where the hell was that?
    I was used to city life.
    Donald and I were not "in love".
    We had a healthy and mature "in like" thing.
    Was that good enough for both of us?
    I packed up and decided to leave.
    Not buy the house.
    Just forget the whole thing.
    Until there was an epiphany.

Friends Gail and Nancy and Donald were sitting in a room and no one spoke.
    "When are you leaving"?

"Tomorrow morning."

Silence.

At that moment, my life stopped.

What was I doing?

What the hell was I doing?

I felt like giving it all up.

All of it.

Donald and I went for a walk.

Daylight, sunny.

We held hands.

Said nothing.

And said everything.

No words, just connection.

In an instant, I got over my foolishness.

I decided to stay.

Someone once said that a real friend is the person you can call at 4AM. And they will be there for you. Donald and Nancy and Gail are real friends. They changed my life. And the people who change our lives can be called cheerleaders. They can be called coaches.

They are precious, rare, gifted.

I began to relax, closed on the house, got myself a PT Cruiser in neon blue, danced at the New Year's Eve party (in dim light so no one saw my uncoordinated feet going in all the wrong directions), and learned that the quality of life starts, once again, when you say YES.

And I listened to myself, not my demons, and found a uniquely wonderful home in a uniquely wonderful place: the Saddle Oak Club, Ocala, Florida.

Playground? You bet.

I say again: you ARE the playground.
Unless you lock yourself out.
Keep the gate wide open.
Magic can happen.
You hold the key.

And I got this from Gail, and Nancy and Donald: we all need a CHEERLEADER and we all need a COACH. We can BE the playground when we realize, once again, that we NEED that playground. Sometimes we must change the channel: stop being an "ass" and go with the natural flow of life.

Cheerleader: I woke up from brain surgery and Chan is sitting at the edge of my bed.

He says to me: "I am no longer your doctor. I am now your cheerleader." Got me going, gave me energy, his energy. Quiet dignified on track energy. He made me see that it was now in my court.

We deserve to have a cheerleader and we are gifted with the sense to be cheerleaders for others. This give and take is a gate to happiness. A "you, too" moment: "I thought I was the only one."

I was sitting with my friend Oscar last night. He is from Turkey.

We talked about the spirit and how to nurture it. We both smiled. We coached each other a bit: how to find the best path for our individual and unique journeys. We were comfortable in our quiet chat. We had only met a few days before. Yet, we knew we could say anything to one another.

COACH: Oscar was mine, I was his for that telling conversation under the trees in the backyard of our retreat house. How to play the "game", how to keep in the game. How to win? Not about winning. It is about SEEING the possibilities.

Let it happen. Be a cheerleader. Be a coach. Be a playground.

COCOON

You can live forever!

You will not die!

You will not get any older!

People loved this film.

For the most part.

It is called "Cocoon."

Picture this:

A huge swimming pool filled with rocks.

A bunch of male friends, all up there in age, invade an off limits pool close to their Florida (where else) retirement community.

A chance to have time off from their usual routine and from the wives.

Nothing unusual yet.

Until the rocks do something for these dudes.

Their energy goes way up.

Their sexual side goes "wow".

Their spirits go from OK to "zing".

The rocks are not just rocks.

You'll have to see the movie to understand why, just to say there is something in those "rocks" creating magic.

The retirees return to their wives and all of a sudden the wives wonder what is going on as libidos have risen, affection is stronger, energy is wild. Happy time!

And then the dilemma: there is a chance to go away from this place and live forever! No illness, no cares, just a happier playground somewhere in a different kind of universe.

Many want to go. Some think this is crazy and refuse to leave. Some DO go.

Fantasy?

Reality?

You decide.

When you "get" that you ARE the playground: what a chance to fill it up with whatever you want. A giant monkey bar to swing from, the water spout to get you wet. You can be anything. A spider, a turtle. Wiggle like a worm.

Spot a cute woman and blush. Spot a cute guy and blush. This can happen at any age.

Infinite space. Infinite possibilities.

It takes imagination. We are born with that.

Sometimes it goes away. Squashed by circumstance. My take on this: get it back.

Be like the wind or the river: go where it needs to go. But GO.

LUBRICATE

The nice thing about all of this: you are in charge. "I am what I am and what I am needs no excuses." A line from the Broadway show "La Cage Aux Folles." A car needs an oil change. A life needs something similar.

Picture a pathway. Muddy, overgrown with weeds, thorny bushes, an old soda can, a cigarette butt, garbage strewn about. Ouch.

Get me out of here.

Now change the picture.

Put in your own form of lubrication to make the path a happy place, one that allows the spirit to flow easily. Rose petals on the ground, a small and unexpected waterfall, a cute squirrel cavorting about, the scent of jasmine, and butterflies of all colors dancing. Blissful.

Since this is your creation: it can be whatever you make it.

And while you are on this path and smiling, HUG A TREE.

OK, have I gone too far?

Just saying: I love to hug trees.

I once got a message from a friend.

He had been pushed too far.

Ready to call it quits. Perhaps.

I wrote back: "I want you to go outside now and hug a tree."

He was the kind of guy who would do it.

No questions asked.

He did.

He sent me a picture of his tree with arms around it.

He was smiling.

Hug a tree.

What does that do for your "playground" self?

First, you are changing the channel. Vital.

The tree feels your hugs.

And you take your time doing this.

You slow down.

You relax the "monkey mind."

You just ARE.

And you turn around and see a squirrel looking at you with wonder.

Enough said.

JETTY TALKS #6

Well, there is a limit.

No, I had no interest in going.

To A Halloween party.

Just stay home and do what?

Better than dressing up.

I never did that as a kid.

Why do it now?

And then I looked around the house and found the makings of a "look" for a party. Had striped John Lennon type pants, a glittery silver vest, purple sunglasses, and nail polish. Tiffany blue nail polish. And rings that I never wore.

Too much? Maybe. But so what.

I had changed my mind and my mood. Off to the club house.

I just decided to go for it.

Kind of breezed in, almost like a dancer.

Saw people I knew and liked.

My take on the look: I am Elton John!

Not what others thought at all.

"Oh, you look so Jimmy Buffett."

I had nothing under the vest.

One woman looked at me as if I were straight on the way to "hell." Oh well. I smiled. Who cares? So what.

Another lady started to play with my chest hair. I knew I would be OK.

Zing!

Sat with friends. And then I got up.

I am challenged when it comes to dancing.

The feet are willing, but they go in the wrong directions sometimes. But I danced!

And then karaoke time. Now this was my thing, although I had never done karaoke, I had done a lot of singing in Broadway style shows in NYC and on tour. So I signed up for karaoke.

Did "Hello, Dolly", the Louis Armstrong version. Chaos! Even the lady who glared at me earlier was applauding. Then "Some Enchanted Evening" from "South Pacific."

Well, that really got them. I love that song: "once you have found her, never let her go." I might have sung "once you have found HIM, never let HIM go." Perhaps I will, another time.

Someone wanted to get me drunk. I am not a drinker. So I knew it was time to leave before doing something stupid.

I went, I had fun, I was Jimmy Buffett. For a few hours.

Takeaway: If some people say "don't", I learned to say "do"! It felt natural. When I see people partying, I am not envious at all. I partied!

SQUIRREL TIME

I love cats and frogs and butterflies and dogs and the occasional squirrel.

My friends and I were sitting outside at a retreat having lunch when this squirrel worked his way onto our table, grabbed the garlic bread (a very large piece) and got away, up his tree. Lovely squirrel food.

That was one happy squirrel. We just roared with laughter. The squirrel had made us happy, too. Give some, get some.

I love cats and dogs and turtles and frogs and the occasional gecko. Must admit: if I could be an animal I would choose to be a cat. A cat knows who he or she is and realizes without any coaching that he or she was born to hunt and to play and to sleep and to get exactly what he or she wants.

And a cat is smarter than a dog. Please do not dislike me for such a thought.

But get this: how many cats would go out and pull a sled in the snow? Dogs love to do that. Cats know they will be cold and uncomfortable and their backs might go out. They pass on that challenge and just sleep.

My favorite cat was called "Bug." Delightful little all black cat. Very intuitive. When my brother tried (and failed) to kill me one day, after I stopped the bleeding Bug climbed onto my chest and just looked at me. I healed quickly. And that cat helped. That is what cats do.

And dogs, too. They are so friendly and needy and funny. Living in NYC for almost 50 years, I got used to dogs. Everywhere. They looked so happy when searching for the perfect place to pee. Glorious relief.

Ever watch a frog?

Frogs are natural athletes. They jump brilliantly. And they stretch. And it is said that frogs are great "lovers." A frog can get attached to another frog and have quite an affair.

And the other frogs do not get jealous at all. Green, perhaps, but not green with envy.

Living creatures of all kinds make me a happier person. Even the occasional snake. If the snake knows his or her place and stays far away from me.

ON A TOMBSTONE:

I Don't
    Get
    Out
    Much
    Anymore

MY DAY IN THE ARMY

I was 21 and it was the time of Vietnam.

Early morning ride to a barracks somewhere.

Nasty, cold looking bus. No one talked.

Into the barracks.

We all were told to strip down.

Just underwear.

What next?

We had to pee into a cup.

I was pee shy.

Nothing came out.

"If you don't do it, you will come back tomorrow" yelled the guy in the uniform.

Somehow I peed.

And then had my banana and sandwich.

And my appointment with the psychiatrist.

He was the most gentle, caring guy I met.

I had checked off "homosexual" tendencies on the intake form.

I almost missed that box.

But it was true.

He looked at me with a fatherly glance.

But he was still stern and no one's fool.

I was glad that I had been myself all day.

One dude dressed up as a woman.

That was probably a big mistake.

"What do you do and where do you do it?".

I had very little experience of the gay world. And I knew I had to tell the absolute truth. And some of it was not a pretty picture.

He listened. His eyes never left mine.

He took a rubber stamp and put it on the intake form.

"You will not be called." Those were his final words to me.

Got back on the same dingy bus.

I did not have an army career.

I was not looking to avoid service.

If I had gone to Vietnam, I would have done my bit.

And why am I even telling you this?

Somehow I was on a good path.

I was not arrogant.

I was not full of ego.

I just played by the rules, told the truth, connected with my true nature, was kind, curious, and showed up.

JETTY TALKS #7

Confidence.

When I ask myself why I'm happy, the road to NOW has been a lot easier for me than for many people I have known. Luck, pure luck, or "mazel" as some friends say, has been abundant.

Example: the night I had brain surgery the team of neurosurgeons was simply perfect. They saved me. No doubt. Luck.

My parents never divorced. Even though it was very "rocky" at the end of their marriage. They saw it out.

I had some very good (and some awful) teachers. The ones who were at the top of their game had no ego. They created a place for us to be curious. And to play.

I have remained an optimist. And I have learned lessons from everyone I have met:

Show up.

Shut up.

Listen better.

Be kind.

Find good in everything.

Be frugal if you need to be.

But never be "cheap."

Praise others.

Smile.

Hold the door open for someone.

Be generous.

Be grateful.

Be yourself.
Do something new each day.
Do something that scares you each day.
Connect with strangers. Make their day.
Happiness bolsters the immune system.
Laugh. And laugh more.
Turn off the news.
Believe in something. Anything.
If in panic mode, hug a tree.
Walk more, even without legs.
Never give up on yourself.
Think young, not old.
Don't retire. Refire.
Be like a cat.
Be like a dog.
Be like a frog.
Paint even if you don't know how.
Dance even if you don't know how.
SAY IT. There is magic in those two words.

PAINTING
ON THE BEACH

John and I went to the beach.
    Took some paint.
    Took a large canvas.
    Windy day.
    Put rocks on the edges of the canvas.
    We did not need to speak.
    Little tubes of acrylic paint.
    Dribbled onto the canvas.
    Lots of colors.
    Pretty colors.
    The wind made the paint swirl around.
    Fun in the sun on a cool day on the beach.
    More paint.
    Stop.
    Smiled.
    What had we done?
    Took the canvas upstairs.
    Let it dry.
    That took a while.

The painting was amazing.
    In one corner there was a cat.
    Another corner, a bird.
    And A fish.

And is that a snake?
Yes.
Nothing planned.
The wind painted the picture.
The beach: a playground.
An artist studio.
A place for quiet creativity.
Together.
Amazing.
Look ma, we made a painting.

JETTY TALKS #8

Someday I might go back to the jetty.
    It is on my "bucket" list.
    But if I do not get there it is OK.
    The jetty is fixed and constant.
    It will never go away.
    And that is how I see it today.
    It is part of me.
    A good, solid part.
    And a thing of beauty and grace.
    Strong, honest, uncomplicated.
    It gave me a sense of freedom.
    I could do anything.
    I became my own playground.
    I played with others.
    I won some, lost some.
    But I can say this: I played.

I was fortunate.
    Some are not so fortunate.
    And I want to tell you a story.
    A story that is very sad, but it is true.
    The story is about a man named Joe.
    1936.
    Joe was good looking.
    He had a sparkle in his eye.
    He was born with limited intelligence.

Spent a lot of his youth in a "facility".
Because he had the IQ of a six year old.
Joe was let out of the "facility."
He was accused of murder.
He was innocent.
But had no verbal ability to defend himself.
Went to prison at age 21.
Sentenced to death.
He was innocent.
But he loved to play.
With his little toy train.
It was his constant companion.
That train made him so happy.
He was asked what he wanted for his last meal.
"Ice cream."
He did not comprehend that he was about to go to the gas
chamber in the prison.
"Please hold my ice cream for later."
He died.
The little train went to his friend.
The warden cried.
72 years later.
Joe was given a posthumous pardon.
He had always been innocent.
I want to be honest:
I am crying right now.
The newspapers called him
The Happiest Man On Death Row.
True to himself. He played.
Right up to the end.

Oh, we have such freedom to BE.
To connect.
To live.
To give back.
To be grateful.
To play.
We need to play.

Apollinaire:
"COME TO THE EDGE," HE SAID.
THEY CAME.
"WE ARE AFRAID."
"COME TO THE EDGE," HE SAID.
THEY CAME.
HE PUSHED THEM.
AND THEY FLEW."

OUR FIELD

"BEYOND THE RIGHTNESS
OR THE WRONGNESS
THERE IS A FIELD.
I'LL MEET YOU THERE."

Rumi

No apologies.
In any book I write, or any talk I give,
I will include the following.
Just saying.
The day is beautiful and bright.
Gentle breeze.
Sunflowers, butterflies roaming.
I go to the field.
I feel like dancing.
I see a big tree in the shade.
And sit down.
Take a large, very ripe strawberry from my pack and
slowly nibble on it.
Sweet.
I close my eyes and drink in the warmth.
I am grateful.
Eyes remain closed.

Suddenly out of nowhere comes my horse.

He looks down at me and is still.

I have never been on a horse.

And I want to ride.

I mount him.

Hold on. Begin to move.

He takes me across the field, gently, with calm resolve. The freedom I feel is palpable. My body becomes part of his body. The energy is electric. I ride and breathe so fully: I want to ride up to the sky. Ride more, breathe more. Live more. Be a kid again.

I feel warm all over. Sounds come out of me. "Ah." "Ah." Take me away. Faster. Please. My horse trots quickly. I hold on. I am euphoric. I am magnificent.

My horse slows down and takes me back to my tree. I dismount and look into the eyes of that gentle giant. Still breathing hard and fully.

I pat my horse's neck slowly and with great care. He whinnies.

And trots away.

Never to be seen by me again.

I WAKE UP FROM MY DREAM.

There is a butterfly on my cheek.

GENEROSITY

We are meant to be givers.

That does not mean we are doormats.

We give because it makes us happy.

It makes others happy.

They need a dollar, we give a dollar.

They need a listener, we listen.

There was a man who lived in my neighborhood in NYC. Nice looking with a calm personality.

He lived in a doorway on the most expensive real estate street in NYC.

He had been there for years. Lumpy mattress, a lot of blankets and comforters,books to read. I asked him one day if he wanted me to bring him more books: "no thanks, I have plenty."

Some would say he had nothing. I say he had what he needed and he was OK.

All in the neighborhood brought him food: good food. He slept in his doorway. He found happiness in his own way. More power to him.

I am so grateful that I do not live in a doorway on a busy street in a noisy city.

Yet, the guy in the doorway taught me something vital: let life take you where it takes you. "Ride the horse in the direction it's going" wrote master life coach Werner Erhard.

The takeaway: ride, play, create, and unleash your talents to make the world a better place. Don't leave this up to others.

If you are a good cook, cook for others.

If you enjoy growing things, let your garden grow.If you love to fish: go fish!

If you want to do something new, work in a fast food place. Ever notice how happy people get in those places? The workers and the customers.

There is a film, "American Beauty", which is not to everyone's taste: it is very, very adult, but most of us can deal with that.

In the film, Kevin Spacey plays an executive who has had enough of corporate life and takes a job in a drive through hamburger place. He just wants to do it. And he has enormous fun.

Talent?

It takes talent to make people happy. The hamburger guy makes you happy. The woman who gives you a bath in the hospital makes you happy. The check out lady in the market makes you happy (usually).

Just unleash those talents. They make a huge difference.

GOOTH!

Get out of the house.

Get off your butt.

SEE things. SAY things. BE things.

CREATE things.

You have the talent.

You are the playground.

You have been all along.

"HAPPINESS
IS ANYONE
AND ANYTHING AT ALL
THAT'S
LOVED BY YOU."

From "You're A Good Man,
 Charlie Brown"
The Musical

APPLAUSE

Who knows. A hundred years from now this book might show up in a "remainder" book shop in Paris. Fun! Hope so.

Thanks to everyone I ever met: the students, the faculty, the strangers on the bus, the people on the trails, my family and John's family, the actors on many stages, the ladies and gentlemen who took care of me in the hospitals, the smiling servers at Taco Bell who put a little extra on my order, the bored servers at Sardi's theater restaurant in NYC who made me feel like a star even when I was not doing a show.

Mrs. Townsend, in fourth grade, taught me the way to be curious. Larry Dilsner, my eccentric and gifted vocal coach, showed me how to sing.

The football team at Long Branch High School showed me how to be more of a man when they "adopted" me in the school cafeteria the time I felt so left out.

The coach made me the team manager (actually a cool changing room janitor). I felt useful. The guys made me feel like I belonged.

Chan Roonprapunt, my surgeon, became a cheerleader and a good friend.

Yet, it was my husband John who truly was my hero, my coach, my forever cheerleader. My anchor. For 46 years. And he never threw me out. John once wrote: "in the middle of a huge pile of garbage, there can be a beautiful red rose."

To you: thanks for reading.
I wish you happiness.
Now, go out and play.
Jay

AUTHOR BIOGRAPHY

Jay Williams earned his PhD while at New York University in Greenwich Village, NYC.

He was Laureate Professor of communications and theater at Kean University. He is an award-winning actor and director. His last book was "Kicked In The Ass Hard, And Still Here." Jay spends time in Europe,and has a cabin in Ocala, Florida, surrounded by enormous oak trees and lots of dancing butterflies. jaytsw@gmail.com

Photo: Topher Frog
Cover Design By TK Palad